W9-BZY-262

HIGH IN THE MOUNTAINS

RUTH YAFFE RADIN

Illustrated by ED YOUNG

Macmillan Publishing Company

New York

Printed and bound in Japan   First American Edition   10 9 8 7 6 5 4 3 2 1

The text of this book is set in 14 point Plantin Light.
The illustrations are rendered in pastels on paper.

Library of Congress Cataloging-in-Publication Data
Radin, Ruth Yaffe.
High in the mountains/Ruth Yaffe Radin;
illustrated by Ed Young.—1st American ed.   p.   cm.
Summary: A young child describes a day spent
near Grandpa's house in the mountains.
ISBN 0-02-775650-5
[1. Mountains—Fiction. 2. Grandfathers—Fiction.]
I. Young, Ed, ill. II. Title.
PZ7.R1216Hi 1989   [E]—dc19
88-13395 CIP AC

To my mother-in-law,

Sophie

—Ruth Yaffe Radin

To Y. N. Yu,

for all the years

of support

—Ed Young

High in the mountains
near Grandpa's house,
there's mostly mist at the start of the day.

It's really the spirits, old folks say,
of those who lived there long ago

and hunted the forests
and fished the waters
and watched the mountain moon at night.

High in the mountains
near Grandpa's house,

I run in a meadow
between the slopes,

Then stop to pick some alpine flowers.

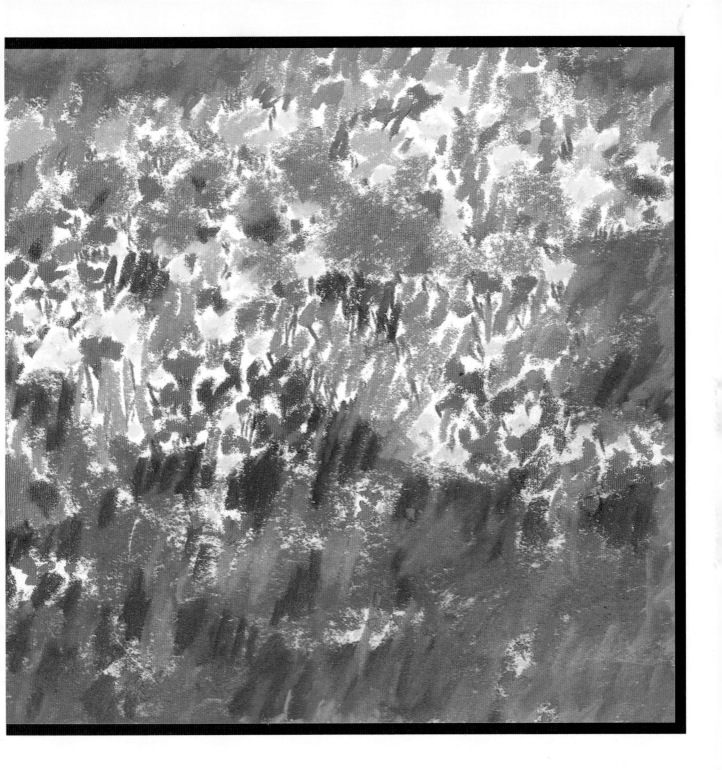

Hiding in between the green,
they can't be seen from far away.

High in the mountains
near Grandpa's house,
there are some boulders, cracked and worn,
that sit so still in quiet ground.

I climb them, watching where I step.
Will they ever tumble downhill,
rolling, rolling, rumbling, rumbling?

High in the mountains
near Grandpa's house,
I watch the deer running and leaping

around the trees—
serious firs stretching tall,
not caring about the deer at all.

High in the mountains
near Grandpa's house,
there is a stream

where water from the melting snow
polishes rocks and sings a song,
lullaby long
on its way to a river far below.
I toss in leaves and watch them go.

High in the mountains
near Grandpa's house,
the afternoon sun touches the peaks

and misses the valleys,
making my shadow very long,
just like a giant lying down.

High in the mountains
near Grandpa's house,
there is a road
that wraps like elastic around each slope.

It is a line that curves and hides
but still connects the near and far,
going higher to the tundra
where no trees can ever grow.

Sometimes Grandpa says,
"Let's go,"

and we pack the car
and follow the road

Up to the clouds, then down again
to a place just right to pitch a tent
facing toward the morning sun.

The air is cool at the end of the day
and we build a fire of twigs and logs.

We watch the flames,
we warm our hands,

And when the fire is dying down
and shadow shapes from sun are gone
and the cricket concert has begun,

We say good-night and go to bed
in sleeping bags, all zipped up,
and think about another day

high in the mountains far away.

RUTH YAFFE RADIN is author of two novels for young readers, *Tac's Island* and *Tac's Turn*. Her previous picture book, *A Winter Place*, illustrated by Mattie Lou O'Kelley, was named a Notable Children's Book by the American Library Association, a Children's Choice by the International Reading Association-Children's Book Council, and a Reading Rainbow Review Book. She and her husband have three children and live in Bethlehem, Pennsylvania.

ED YOUNG was born in Tientsin, China, and now lives with his wife, Filomena, in Hastings-on-Hudson, New York. He has illustrated more than thirty books for children, including *The Emperor and the Kite* by Jane Yolen (a 1968 Caldecott Honor Book), *Yen Shen: A Cinderella Story from China* by Ai-Ling Louie (a 1983 *Boston Globe-Horn Book* Honor Award), and his own *Up a Tree* (a 1983 *New York Times* Best Illustrated Book). Recent titles include *In the Night, Still Dark* by Richard Lewis, *Eyes of the Dragon* by Margaret Leaf, and *Whale Song* by Tony Johnston.